Emmy
the Exaggerating
Elephant

Fenton
the Fearful Frog

Gertie
the Grungy Goat

Ivy
the Happy
Hamster

Ivy
the Impatient
Iguana

Ollie
the Obedient
Ostrich

Perry
the Polite
Porcupine

Queenie
the Quiet Quail

Rupert
the Resourceful
Rhinoceros

Wendy
the Wise
Woodchuck

Xavier
the X-ploring
Xenops

Yori
the Yucky Yak

Ziggy
the Zippy Zebra

NOTE TO PARENTS

Queenie's Secret
A story about the benefit of quiet contemplation

In this story, the AlphaPets are curious about Queenie the Quiet Quail. They are convinced that she must have a special secret because she's always so quiet and seems so contented. One day, in order to find out her secret, the AlphaPets follow her wherever she goes. In doing so, they inadvertently find out about the many satisfactions that quiet activities and contemplation can bring.

In addition to enjoying this story with your child, you can use it to teach a gentle lesson about the pleasure of quiet times and solitary play. Help your child understand that while noisy games with friends and loud music may be fun, working and playing alone also has its rewards.

You can also use this story to introduce the letter **Q**. As you read about Queenie the Quiet Quail, ask your child to listen for all the words that start with **Q** and point to the objects that begin with **Q**. Explain that **Q** is usually followed by **u** in the English language. When you've finished reading the story, your child will enjoy doing the activity at the end of the book.

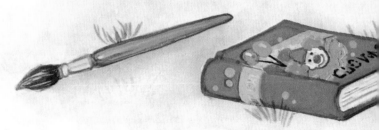

The AlphaPets™ characters were conceived and created by Ruth Lerner Perle.
Characters interpreted and designed by Deborah Colvin Borgo.
Cover/book design and production by Norton & Company.
Logo design by Deborah Colvin Borgo and Nancy S. Norton.
Printed and Manufactured in the United States of America

Queenie's Secret

RUTH LERNER PERLE

Illustrated by Judy Blankenship

Danbury, Connecticut

One day, some of the AlphaPets went down to the lake to play.

"Let's play baseball!" said Delilah the Demanding Duck.

"Nah! I'm tired of playing ball," cried Sylvester the Stubborn Squirrel. "I'd rather jump rope."

"I don't feel like jumping rope," said Ivy the Impatient Iguana. "How about a game of Frisbee?"

"No, we always play Frisbee!" said Ziggy the Zippy Zebra. "*Everything* is boring."

The AlphaPets dropped their things on the ground and started to toss pebbles into the lake.

On the other side of the lake, Queenie the Quiet Quail was fishing at the water's edge.

"Look at Queenie!" shouted Vinnie the Vocal Vulture. "She looks as if *she's* having fun!"

"But why is she always so quiet," said Sylvester.

"Maybe she's quiet because she's shy," said Ziggy.

"Maybe she's quiet because she's hiding a secret," said Delilah.

"Yes, indeed! What could her secret be?" asked Vinnie.

"I don't know!" whooped Delilah, "but I sure would like to find out. Let's follow Queenie and see what she does all day. Then maybe we'll learn her secret."

The AlphaPets continued throwing stones into the lake until they saw Queenie get up to leave.

"Here's our chance!" Vinnie whispered. "Let's go!"

Everybody followed Queenie out of the park, across the street, and into the library.

Queenie walked from bookcase to bookcase. The AlphaPets followed quietly behind her.

Queenie pretended not to know that her AlphaPet friends were following her. She just smiled a gentle smile and continued to look at books.

"Hmm . . . I wonder if Queenie's secret is hidden in these books," Sylvester said.

Queenie picked two books from the shelf, checked them out, and left the library.

Ziggy also took a book from the shelf. "This book will be fun to read. I think I'll borrow it," he said.

"I'll take one too," Delilah said.

"Hurry!" Ivy called. "We don't want to lose Queenie."

After checking out their books, the AlphaPets followed Queenie home.

"Maybe, just maybe, we'll discover her secret now," Vinnie said.

The AlphaPets hid behind a bush and watched quietly as Queenie went into her flower garden. She picked bluebells, daisies, irises, tulips, and peonies.

"What beautiful spring flowers!" Sylvester whispered. "Growing those takes a lot of work! Maybe I should spend more time tending my garden."

Queenie went back into the house and arranged her bouquet in a glass vase. Then she went out to the porch and painted a beautiful picture of her flower arrangement.

"Hey! That's terrific," Ziggy whispered. "I never knew Queenie was an artist— and a talented one, too!"

Queenie left her painting to dry and went out to feed the birds. As soon as she opened her bag of birdseed, dozens of brightly colored birds came flying overhead.

"Just look at those birds!" Ivy whispered. "They don't seem afraid of Queenie at all. What fun she's having!"

Queenie could hear the AlphaPets whispering, but she just smiled gently.

When all the birdseed was gone, Queenie went into her house and brought out her silver flute. She played a lovely melody. Behind her, the AlphaPets swayed to the rhythm of the music.

Soon Queenie went back into the house. The AlphaPets watched as she made six sandwiches. "That's a lot of sandwiches!" Vinnie whispered. "I wonder who they're for."

Queenie just smiled and put the sandwiches into a picnic basket with some plates, cups, napkins, and a quart of milk. Then she walked out the back door.

The AlphaPets ran to the back of the house and hid behind the bushes.

"We've been watching Queenie all day, but we still don't know her secret!" Delilah complained.

"Ssh!" Ziggy said. "Here comes Queenie now."

Queenie spread a big quilt on the ground beside the quince tree. She poured herself a cup of milk and ate one of the sandwiches.

"I'm getting hungry," Ivy said.

"So am I," said Sylvester. The others nodded their heads in agreement.

Queenie peeked over at the bushes and smiled.

Then she stretched out on her stomach and quietly stared down at the ground.

Vinnie stared down at the ground too. "What's Queenie looking at? What is there to see here?" he wondered. "All I see is grass and twigs."

Then Vinnie noticed something move under the grass. He looked closer. There were hundreds of tiny ants carrying breadcrumbs from the quilt to their anthill.

"Well, I'll be!" he said under his breath. "If that's not the snake's slippers! The king's wings! The bee's knees! Who would ever guess that these tiny critters were working away right here under my very nose!"

Ziggy and Ivy also looked down into the grass. Ivy saw tiny red berries hiding under a clump of zig-zag-edged leaves.

"I know what these are!" cried Ivy as she picked a berry. "These are wild strawberries and they smell delicious!" Ivy picked another little berry and gave it to Ziggy to smell.

They continued looking in the grass and discovered dozens of violets growing from a patch of shiny round leaves.

Ziggy put a violet in his buttonhole. Then he picked a bunch for Ivy.

"Oh, thank you," Ivy said as she smelled their perfume.

Queenie lay on her back and looked up at the sky.

Sylvester and Delilah looked up too. There were puffs of clouds in the sky. They looked like giant cottonballs floating in a big blue sea.

As the day came to a close, everyone watched the sunset. Yellow and red sunbeams were shining through the cloud puffs. They reminded Delilah of crepe paper party decorations. They reminded Sylvester of magic dragons riding in the sky.

Soon the sun sank behind the trees and the sky grew dark.

Queenie built a little campfire. Smiling a gentle little smile, she straightened her quilt and laid out five sandwiches and cups of milk. She motioned to her friends to join her. Silently, the AlphaPets crept over and sat down on Queenie's quilt. They each smiled a gentle little smile and gave her a warm hug.

Everything was quiet except for the crackle of the fire and the AlphaPets munching their sandwiches.

The AlphaPets watched in silence as thousands of stars sparkled in the night sky.

Then the moon appeared—a crescent quarter smiling down at them.

But the moon and the stars weren't the only twinklers in the night. Soon there were hundreds of fireflies darting back and forth, back and forth, among the swaying quince blossoms.

One by one, the AlphaPets closed their eyes and fell fast asleep.

But soon Queenie heard a funny noise. She sat up and looked around. All her friends were sleeping peacefully— except for Vinnie. He was talking in his sleep. "Yes, indeed," he said. "If I said it once I said it a thousand times, there's nothing like a little peace and quiet. That must be Queenie's secret. Yes, indeed!"

Queenie smiled a gentle smile and gave each of the AlphaPets a kiss on the cheek. Then, ever so softly, she whispered, "Be still, dear friends, sleep tight. Good night!"

Please whisper these words with me.

quince

question mark

quarter

queen

quilt

quart

Look back at the pictures in this book and find these and other words that begin with Q.

Know Your Alphabet

Aa Bb

Gg Hh

Mm Nn Oo Pp

Uu Vv Ww

Emmy
the Exaggerating
Elephant

Fenton
the Fearful Frog

Gertie
the Grungy Goat

the Happy
Hamster

the Impatient
Iguana

Ollie
the Obedient
Ostrich

Perry
the Polite
Porcupine

Queenie
the Quiet Quail

Rupert
the Resourceful
Rhinoceros

Wendy
the Wise
Woodchuck

Xavier
the X-ploring
Xenops

Yori
the Yucky Yak

Ziggy
the Zippy Zebra

NOTE TO PARENTS

<u>Xavier and the Laughing Xoxos</u>
A story about the pleasure of new experiences

In this story, Xavier the X-ploring* Xenops convinces his AlphaPet friends to take a trip to Hawaii. Though many are reluctant at first, Xavier—with the help of the mythical Laughing Xoxos, shows his friends that adventures and new experiences can bring pleasure and satisfaction.

In addition to enjoying this story with your child, you can use it to teach a gentle lesson about the rewards of keeping an open mind, appreciating unfamiliar things, and looking for the value in life experiences.

You can also use this story to introduce the letter **X**. As you read about Xavier the X-ploring Xenops, ask your child to listen for all the sounds that **X** makes in words, and to point to the objects that have that sound somewhere in their names. When you've finished reading the story, your child will enjoy doing the activity at the end of the book.

* Artistic license was taken in the spelling of Xavier's characteristic attribute.

The AlphaPets™ characters were conceived and created by Ruth Lerner Perle.
Characters interpreted and designed by Deborah Colvin Borgo.
Cover/book design and production by Norton & Company.
Logo design by Deborah Colvin Borgo and Nancy S. Norton.
Printed and Manufactured in the United States of America

Xavier and the Laughing Xoxos

RUTH LERNER PERLE

Illustrated by Judy Blankenship

One day, some of the AlphaPets went to Xavier the X-ploring Xenops's house. Xavier showed them his collection of souvenirs from all the places he had been.

"Where are you going next?" Emmy the Exaggerating Elephant asked.

"I've been reading all about Hawaii. It's way out in the Pacific Ocean," Xavier answered. "How would you all like to come along with me?"

"I don't know," Fenton the Fearful Frog said. "It's awfully far away from home."

"That's exactly the point, Fenton!" Xavier said. "Hawaii *is* far away. There would be lots of wonderful new things to see and do."

"If we go to a faraway place, how will we know the right things to do?" Perry the Polite Porcupine asked.

"Finding out is half the fun! That's what exploring is all about!" Xavier said.

Emmy thought for a while. "Maybe Xavier is right. I'll go along," she said.

"I'll go, too," Justin the Joking Jackal said, looking at Emmy. "Just for laughs."

"So will I," Delilah the Demanding Duck said. "But it had better be fun, Xavier, or else!"

"I promise you'll have fun," Xavier said.

Everybody agreed to go.

Finally it was the day of the big trip. Perry and Xavier were the first ones to arrive at the airport. Then came Delilah, Justin, and Fenton.

"Where's Emmy?" Delilah asked. "She'd better hurry or she'll miss the plane."

Just then the AlphaPets saw a mountain of luggage coming their way. It was Emmy pushing a cart filled with sixteen big suitcases, six duffel bags, and a large hat box.

"Hi, everybody!" she called. "I'm sooo excited I can hardly wait to get to Hawaii!"

"What are we waiting for? Let's go!" whooped Xavier.

As soon as they boarded the plane, Fenton started to worry. "What if my luggage gets lost?" he said. "What if it rains every day we're there?"

"These seats are too narrow!" Emmy complained as she tried to buckle her seat belt.

"I hope this trip won't be too long," Delilah said.

"Or too boring," Justin added.

"Will we get something to eat?" Perry wanted to know. "I'm hungry."

"Try to relax, everybody!" Xavier said. "We'll get a meal right after we take off, and then we'll see a movie!"

Just then the engine started, and the plane took off.

"Yippee! We're on our way!" Xavier cried. "Look out your windows, everybody! Houses and cars look like toys from up here. And the roads look like ribbons."

But the AlphaPets were too uncomfortable to look.
Justin and Emmy felt too warm. Delilah and Perry
felt too cold. And Fenton was too busy reading the
emergency instructions.

Xavier looked out of his window and watched as the
plane flew toward the sun, through puffy white clouds,
and over mountain peaks.

"I wish my friends were having a better time," he
thought. "I hope they'll have fun when we get to Hawaii."

When the plane landed at Honolulu International Airport, everybody was tired and cranky.

"My dress is all rumpled, and my foot is asleep," Emmy said.

"At least your foot fell asleep. I was so uncomfortable, I couldn't sleep a wink," complained Delilah.

"Don't be upset, you'll feel better when we get to the hotel," Xavier said.

After they collected their baggage, the AlphaPets piled into a big taxi.

"Welcome to our island," said the driver. "We're off to the magical, mysterious Xanadu Hotel!"

"What's magical and mysterious about it?" Fenton asked.

"The Xanadu was built near the foot of the Mauna Loa Volcano," the driver explained. "Long ago, the ancient tribe of Laughing Xoxos lived near Mauna Loa. It is said that their spirits are still there today, helping those who believe in having fun and adventure."

The AlphaPets rode on in silence, wondering what the next few days would bring.

When they arrived at the Xanadu Hotel Emmy said, "I'm starving! Let's get something to eat!"

"Good idea!" said Delilah. "I want a peanut butter and jelly sandwich."

"I'd like a hamburger and french fries," Perry said.

"Pizza for me!" Justin added.

So the AlphaPets went into the restaurant. They looked at all the exotic food laid out on the long table, but there was no peanut butter sandwich, no hamburger, and no pizza.

Everyone groaned with disappointment as their stomachs growled with hunger.

"Oh, dear, oh, dear!" Fenton sighed. "I hope the Laughing Xoxos can help make things better here."

That gave Xavier an idea. "I know just what to do to make my friends enjoy this adventure," he thought.

"I think coming here may have been a mistake after all," Delilah said.

"It's been a long day. Let's go to bed," Perry suggested. "Maybe we'll feel better in the morning."

"You go ahead without me. I'll be up soon," Xavier said. "I want to read a little more and finish my soda."

"Let us know if you see one of the Laughing Xoxos!" Justin called with a chuckle as he went upstairs.

Early the next morning, Xavier woke his friends. "Let's go to the beach so we can see the sun rise!" he said.

The AlphaPets got dressed and followed Xavier to the beach. As they walked along the water's edge, Perry pointed to something bobbing on the water.

"Hey! I wonder what that is!" Delilah shouted as she waded out to get it. "Look, it's a bottle! And there's a note inside!" she said, handing the bottle to Xavier. Xavier took the note out of the bottle, and read it aloud.

Hee, hee, hee! Hoo, hoo, hoo!
Be sure to enjoy whatever you do.
Ha, ha, ha! Ho, ho, ho!
Laugh and smile wherever you go.
All you explorers—ready or not
Follow along where X marks the spot!
Signed, X

"That X must be the sign of the Laughing Xoxos!" Fenton said. "We'd better do what they say!"

The sun was up by now
and the AlphaPets could see
a yellow note tacked to the
coconut palm. They ran over
to see what it said.

**Climb a tree, pick a nut,
Eat it in a thatched straw hut
Signed, X**

So everyone climbed up a
palm tree. Everyone except
Fenton, that is.

"Whee! This is fun!"
Emmy shouted.

When they came down
again, they cracked the
coconuts open and ate the
delicious fresh nut meat.

"Yummy! I never knew
coconuts were so sweet and
crunchy," Delilah said.

CLIMB A TREE,
PICK A NUT,
EAT IT IN A
THATCHED
STRAW HUT
X

The next note was at the boat house. It read:

Get some goggles, go below
See a bright and lively show!
                    Signed, X

Everybody ran to get flippers and diving goggles. Then they jumped into the water.

The AlphaPets could hardly believe their eyes! There were hundreds of brightly colored fish and other sea creatures swimming all around them!

"Wow! I've never seen anything like this," said Emmy. "It's wonderful . . . marvelous . . . spectacular!"

When they returned to the boat house, they noticed another note which read:

You've been below—you're very brave
Now rent a board and catch a wave.
Signed, X

"Hurray! That means surfing!" Xavier shouted. So they all carried their surfboards to the edge of the sea. At first they kept slipping off into the water. But they kept trying and trying until finally everybody could float on their boards. Everybody including Fenton.

"If we had more time, we could even learn to stand on these boards!" he said with a happy smile.

The AlphaPets were so busy having fun that they had no time to be tired, or worried, or grumpy like before.

The next few days were filled with more new and wonderful adventures. Following instructions that were left along the way, the AlphaPets visited a live volcano and watched the smoke coming out at the top. "That's hot stuff!" Justin giggled.

They went to a plantation and picked pineapples. "I thought pineapples grew on trees," Perry said as he picked one from the spiky-looking plant.

Then they loaded sugar cane on an oxcart and rode it to the sugar factory. "Making sugar is more fun than eating it!" Emmy declared.

On their last day in Hawaii, the AlphaPets went to visit the tropical rain forest. There were giant plants and flowers growing everywhere, and hundreds of animals watching them as they walked on the forest floor.

Everyone was having a wonderful time, especially Xavier. He was so happy his friends were enjoying their wonderful adventure.